MOON BITTEN

A DARK AND TWISTED FAIRY TALE

ANGHARAD THOMPSON REES

"Be careful," Blaxton warns.

I pull the hood of my red cape over my head, concealing myself against the gust of frigid winds biting with ice and spite. The sky hold the promise of more snow to come. He does not let go of my hand. And it's not the snow concerning him.

"Blaxton," I say—his name as sweet as honey on my recently-kissed lips. "Do not concern yourself. It is but a short walk through the woods, and yes, I promise to stay on the tracks."

I raise an eyebrow, threatening him to contradict me. But he should know my penchant for wandering and losing myself. That's how we met—deep within the woods during the first days of spring, when frost thawed atop the lake and his green eyes melted ice from my nervous heart.

He pulls me into his chest, his body warm against my own, tempting me to stay. Tempting me to never leave. I melt into him, lips hot as the first flakes of snow dance from the sky.

"Blaxton, no," I say, pulling myself away with reluctance. The space between his heart and mine gapes as if the very universe could fill the hole. "I have to get back to Grandma, you know I do."

His face drops at her mention. Grandma despises him despite his soft features, warm honey eyes and sweet, crooked smile. Though I suspect her hatred is aimed more at the threat he will steal me from her. Just as her daughter, my mother, was stolen so many years ago I can no longer picture her face. But that was different. Mother did not fall in love as I have. She was taken…

By wolves.

A perfectly timed howl echoes across the valley, carried along the land muted by snow. Blaxton raises his own eyebrow at the beast's call and I laugh. An empty tin-like sound of hollow mirth and creeping fear.

"I'll be fine. Tomorrow," I say, allowing a smile

to creep across my frost-numb face. "Let's meet tomorrow, same time and place."

Blaxton captures loose strands of my red hair in his pale fingers. The contrast startling like blood on snow. Tucking the strands behind my left ear, his fingers trail my cheek as he kisses my forehead. "Tomorrow," he promises. "But... Woolsey will be here."

I tense. There is something about his friend, the way he looks at me, that sets me on edge—makes my stomach coil within itself.

Blaxton's face pulls into an apologetic grimace. "Don't worry, I'll change plans. I'll think of something, so it's just you and me."

And I know he will. He always does.

There are not many things in the world harder than leaving Blaxton behind, but I don't look back as my feet crunch on snow hardened by late afternoon frost. For there are other things to worry about, other things keeping me focused on getting home before nightfall. Such as the strange deaths accumulating in the village by the day, or should I say, night. Bodies found mutilated and gnawed, limbs missing, necks ravaged.

My pace quickens, as much as the deepening

snow will allow, and I ignore its cruel bite gnawing from my feet to my ankles. Toes already numb. And all I hear is the deep silence of the snow-laden land-scape—my lone steps and heavy breath as I break into an ungainly jog. I wish at this point, to be a skipping fox, and perhaps that's how I may look if eyes watched my red cape fluttering against the white snow from a distance. But the eyes I feel upon me do not feel distant. They feel close and hungry and perhaps I am making this up with fear and folly.

The deaths.

A lone wolf's howl.

The gossip; *what if the lone wolf has returned? It took Red's mother all them eons ago. Perhaps it has come back to take her too?* Overheard conversations and supersti-tious nonsense.

But still, I break into a sprint as Grandma's cottage comes into view.

SOUNDS TRAVEL DIFFERENTLY UPON SNOW. It's as if the entire world sleeps while each step a crude yell. Each breath a rasping heave.

There is neither birdsong nor the rustling of leaves overhead. A deeper silence perhaps than silence itself. So when Grandma's scream bellows from the cottage in the distance, the sound races towards me like a raging storm.

I charge along the path, despite fear weakening my bowels. But it's not only her scream pulling my heart downwards towards my pounding feet, but the snarling growls and malicious yelps accompanying her cries for help. Somewhere, in the back of my mind, the place locked deep within my subconscious, I've heard those sounds before. A memory too painful to hold, too cruel to remember. Mother's sacrifice to save me while I was mere bairn.

I snap that memory back into its box as I race up the wooden steps of the veranda. A strange moment to notice the blue paint flaking from the walls exposing patches of tired, rotting oak. A stranger time still to notice the flower boxes empty and barren save from frost-touched soil as dark as death. Another step and I burst through the door already ajar.

It's the heat that first hits me, the raging warmth of the roaring fireplace hot against my cold, cold cheeks.

And then the blood.

"Grandma!" I scream, an awful primal sound raging from the deepest depths of my soul.

Both she and the wolf pause for a microsecond, all eyes on mine. Grandma's scrunched up pain-ridden eyes are filled with a deep fear. Blood smears the entire right side of her face. The wolf's amber eyes stare with bottomless hunger and rage.

"Run, Red! *Run!*" Grandma yells. Her wail jolts the beast back into its savage attack with a yelp of frustration. But I do not run. Cannot. I stand, stunned—silent as forgotten secrets as the pair wrestle on the ground in a blur of white fur and fang. Grandma's grey hair is stained as red as mine as she rolls and struggles through puddles of blood on a threadbare rug.

And finally, my body springs into action and my thoughts disappear.

Fur is warm within my clutches. Hard, lean muscles beneath my palms. Teeth snap. Warm musky breath—with the metallic twang of Grandma's blood—hits my face. I roar, grappling to pull the beast away. It barks in anger, and mauls my arm. Fangs splitting skin, bone and sinew. And I howl, recoiling for but a moment before I launch at it again. This time, the beast charges at me, slamming me onto my back. It growls and yelps, and for a moment I am glad its blood-stained fangs gnash inches from my face for it allows Grandma to save herself. But she doesn't move, no matter how much I will her to stand. To run. To live.

The wolf grabs at my wounded arm as I protect my face with my hands, its teeth puncturing skin once more. The pain is exquisite, a sensation reminding me how fragile souls are trapped within our breakable bodies. And I see nothing but those glowing amber eyes. The twilight hour has crept through the windows and doors, and the crackling fire glows brighter in the descending darkness.

Above me, the wolf's shadow looms high and large on the wall, flickering with the flames as I flicker from conscious thought to nothing but the sensation of fangs sinking into my flesh.

Time passes. I lose myself in a black hole of nothing—no pain, no fear.

The grandfather clock chimes, waking me with a start and rousing my consciousness.

The pain and fear now double.

The wolf is no longer above me. It grapples over Grandma's body once more. Blood covers the beast's white fur and a furless black scar akin to a question mark follows the animal's spine. But the only question I can think of is will Grandma survive this vicious attack?

The clock chimes again, a deathly *tick tock*, counting down the seconds of Grandma's life.

Crimson stains my fingers, a warm thick fluid chilling my heart as I scramble to my hands and knees. There's no time, despite another chime. There's nothing I can do to save her. I'm too late. Too weak…

"You can never have her," Grandma moans. Resilient, even as she stares death, and the savage wolf, in the face.

A guttural howl explodes, dancing from the

walls and low ceiling of the cottage; trapped—like Grandma under the wolf's fierce claws. Trapped, like me, paralysed in my body as I brace against a noise I cannot escape—the curdling of Grandma's blood stuck in her ravaged throat as she dies.

I clamber to my feet, rage propelling me to the small kitchen bench. A knife is in my hands before I have time to think, and I launch myself at the white beast speckled with red. The knife slices straight through its flesh and muscles as easily as puncturing an overripe fruit. It howls—a grotesque sound full of fury and anguish. The beast knocks me down, turns and lopes away, leaving me rasping on the floor—the knife still wedged in its flesh.

I take one look at Grandma's dead body and wish I hadn't. And then, with no reason to stay, I pursue the wolf into the darkness.

3

Darkness wraps itself around me, and despite the low set moon offering little light, it is not hard to follow the wolf's path. The red stains in the snow are like some gruesome fairy-tale trail leading to a house made of gingerbread or some other cruel witch's abode. And I wonder where this wolf will lead me.

Perhaps to my death.

My wound pulses to the rhythm of my feet slowed only by the depth of new snowfall. A squeaking softness now, a sound like chewing cotton wool, a God awful sound for a God awful night. And though I should not curse, what else is there to do? Wolves have killed my mother and grandma both and I can only believe it *is* a curse.

I continue following the bloody paw prints and speckles of blood leaking from the knife wound. Through the woods I track the beast, where trees loom over me, their skeletal branches laden with snow grasping at my very soul. Over the frozen timid brook I follow, hoping my weight will not break the cold touch of ice and frost and hopelessness, and send me crashing into the water that dares flow beneath the surface.

I freeze. Short, shallow breaths balloon in front of my face. My wound smarts in the cold. I grasp it, and squat to inspect the paw prints on the ground. Next to them rests my knife, tip first in the bloody snow. I pick it up while considering the paw prints —they're changing, elongating, morphing.

I can only assume the beast is faltering, slowing —unsteady on its weakening limbs. Good. Perhaps the one knife wound was all it needed. But this thought does not bring me relief or joy as I continue to stalk, because the prints are morphing still, and this time it is undeniable.

They have turned into human footsteps…

And the footsteps lead directly towards Blaxton's homestead.

There are moments in life when reality and fantasy combine, and for several fractions of a second, I suspend my disbelief and consider the possibility of what my eyes can see but mind can't fathom. Nothing makes sense but the erratic beat of my heart hammering against my ribcage. The footsteps do not go to the door, but around the house to the barns and stables. A deeper concern now surfaces.

Blaxton.

I cannot lose the only two people I love in one night.

Neither candlelight nor fire in the hearth shines from the windows of Blaxton's homestead. Instead, the wooden dwelling seems to place a finger over its mouth of a door and whispers an urgent *shhh*. My clumsy frozen toes stumble up the three steps, and the crash in the otherwise silent night sends a murder of ravens cawing into the nighttime sky. They soon settle back onto branches of the old oak that hovers over the house. And they watch me, waiting, perhaps, for their spoils. In the summer, the old oak looks like a safe warm promise. Tonight, with its empty spindly branches, and a murder coolly considering me, it looks only like a threat.

I rap on the door, though I am certain Blaxton is not inside.

"Blaxton," I whisper, because on a night like

this, a whisper is all I have. "Blaxton?" And I learn even a whisper can sound urgent and desperate.

A howl, ravage and wild, cuts through my thoughts.

My eyes clench and I clutch at my wound, blood seeping between my fingers. Nausea grows to my throat, and I breathe a measured breath to gather myself.

Forget the pain, I urge myself. Forget Grandma's pale and lifeless eyes. Forget…

A scream slices through the air. The ravens scatter, black wings and feathers. This time they do not return—the murder taking place elsewhere. Another scream, and I spin around, and around again. The sound echoes across the valley and it's hard to discern from which direction. And in that moment, with the kitchen knife still clutched in my hand, I wonder whether I should be running towards or away from the scream that cries out one last time.

A gunshot.

A thud.

I need to breathe but fear grips my throat like cruel fingers.

Footsteps stalk behind me. I have to dare myself to look around, but cannot.

I have to rouse myself to raise the knife, but I do not.

The footsteps near and I can neither distinguish if they belong to man nor beast.

I count down from three, steel myself and spin towards my stalker.

The knife clatters to the ground and I scream.

4

I BACK AWAY AND stumble over a log basket, sending firewood spilling across the veranda. The front door balances me, stopping me before I fall.

"Blaxton?" I whimper, a sick sound even in my own troubled mind.

He reaches for me, though he is nowhere near touching distance. I want him to stop. I *need* him to stop, right there, and not come any closer. But words stick in my throat and all I can do is shake my head under my red hooded cape.

He is covered in blood, from head to toe, and he is not alone. Beside Blaxton stalks Woolsey, he too is blooded yet he smiles at me in a way that makes me back further against the wooden door already pressed hard against my back. And I can't fathom my own thoughts because what I think cannot be true.

Blaxton reaches the steps and his friend has the decency at least to wait below. Still, I feel cornered.

"What… What?" I stutter, cursing myself for my incoherence. But I can't piece the parts together.

The paw prints turning to footprints. The howl. The scream. The gunshot and the blood.

"Red?" he asks, and the softness of his voice makes me see, truly see, what is in front of me. White tracks stream down his blooded checks from his eyes. He's crying. And I take his out stretched hands.

"The old mare, Betsy," he said, shaking his head. "The wolf, it got to her, she didn't stand a chance—mauled her in seconds. I was there, I tried to fight it off and if it wasn't for Woolsey suddenly turning up from nowhere when he did…"

He turns to his friend who has yet to take his hungry eyes from me. I spare Woolsey a quick glance, and subconsciously my eyes trail to his side. There is no knife wound, no blood, and I chastise myself for thinking the impossible.

Things slowly begin to make sense, pieces of the puzzle beginning to fit. The howls. The screams belonged to poor Betsy, the lovely old carthorse who was as soft as she was strong. But her strength would have been no match for a vicious attack. There are many types of strengths, after all.

"The gunshot?" I ask, because I need to know to set my wandering mind back onto the correct path.

"That was me," Woolsey says and I detect more than a hint of pride to his supercilious tone. "The mare was dying in agony. I shot her, and the wolf disappeared out of sight."

Blaxton nodded, agreeing with the tale that sets my chattering teeth on edge. Then his blood stained face morphs into a different expression. He notices my blood, my paler than pale complexion, the not rightness of my being here in the dark, in the snow, and his own thoughts of wolves and Betsy are overtaken. I can see it by the way his honey eyes melt.

"What's happened? What—" he grabs me into his warm body. "What happened to you?"

And I want to tell him. I want to tell him everything. The fight. Grandma dead. My wound. The knife in the wolf's side. The changing paw prints in the snow.

But the bite mark pulls all of my thoughts into those puncture wounds, like my entire self is now

centred around those four marks leaking crimson
onto Blaxton's pale, white hands. A startling
contrast I have seen before when life was neither
gruesome nor painful.

The pain grips me, pulls me, yanks me from my
body and mind. I drop, feeling the scattered logs
digging awkwardly into my body as I tumble
deeper.

"Red?" I hear Blaxton call but his voice sounds
so far away.

"What the hell?" I hear Woolsey, a tone full of
anger that also fades away. Their heated voices
dissolve into background muffled sounds—then
silence.

And for me, my mind goes as blank as the snow-
filled landscape. There is nothing but a void, and I
tumble down its gaping hole.

INTERLUDE – WHITE HOT

Ice white fills my veins—a freezing burn blazing through the labyrinth of my body. It twists and turns through the million minuscule tunnels crisscrossing from brain to heart to lung and sinew. And there is nowhere to escape the sensation. Nowhere to escape the pain. It grips my heart in a vice, squeezing the life from me but I cannot yell out. I am not here, yet experience it all the same. The pulling, the purging, the persistent grab of claws and fangs. The only place that does not pulsate in agony is the four puncture wounds beckoning me to solace. The four tiny spaces I try to crawl into, to find peace and sanctuary from the burning madness. I just want to stay here, in these four tiny spaces. Safe from the pain.

5

I have passed out many times since the attack, and the dreams only get worse. I call them dreams because the real nightmare begins when I open my eyes. The stark truth as blinding as the winter sun blazing on the crystal-tipped snow before me.

To my right is a pile of black soil. It must have been a hellish job for the gravediggers in the hard frost of winter. The undertaker said she would keep —Grandma—she would keep, because the weather was so cold. And I could not help myself but to think of a pail of milk sitting on the kitchen counter. She would say the same thing in the winter, *it will keep a long while yet before it spoils.* But I didn't want Grandma to spoil any further than she already had; to curdle or go bitter or grow mould on her mangled skin and flesh. So, no, I told the under-taker, she will not keep, she will be buried, and here I am, watching the cheap timber coffin—the best I could afford—lower into the ground.

Blaxton squeezes my hand, though I wish he wouldn't. I can barely contain my grief and any ounce of care or concern or pity cast my way could break the dam walls and my tears would flood the land, though I doubt it would thaw the snow or my thoughts. So I busy myself with distractions and look around at the mournful faces of the few who knew the body sinking into the depths. She was old, too old to have many friends. She had already seen them pass. What is left are the relatives of once friends, people of goodwill who wish to support a woman who earned so much respect in the village, and the *others*. The others who have come to watch the spectacle—to watch me. The lone survivor of the lone wolf's attack that has taken my mother and hers too.

They think I can't see through the facade of pity, but I feel it all right. Their darting, nervous eyes. Their whispers behind black silken gloves and shifting eyes veiled beneath black lace. But for all the people to show, it's Woolsey who irks me the most. He, with his pack of friends pretending to show respect. Woolsey stares at me, his eyes gorging over my body. I do not give him the satisfaction of returning his gaze—but I do stare down the girl hovering tightly to his left. The peculiar creature glares at me with her beautiful sharp features, her striking eyes; one gold one blue. She all but snarls, taking a possessive step closer to the boy whose eyes have not left my own. Her siblings step forward, six, maybe seven boys ranging from ten to twenty years old, silently warning me to back down from their sister.

I feel exposed, suddenly vulnerable. So I squeeze Blaxton's hand and for a small moment, I feel safe.

People asked me if I wanted to hold a wake for Grandma, but I decided against it, for there is nothing *awake* about the dead. And I feel mourning is a private thing, best savoured for lonely, solo moments when the world cannot see the tears or hear my howls of grief as I kneel, broken, on the threadbare rug that still bears Grandma's dried blood. I haven't washed out the stain and I do not intend to—really, it is the only thing I have left of her, any *real* tangible thing, because memories cannot be touched and therefore do not count.

The funeral party—if such a gathering can be

referred to as a party—disperses and the gossip begins to circulate as the good people line neatly behind one another to wait their turn to tell me how very sorry they are, and how they are here for me if I ever need anything. But I hear the others, the whispers that are not so much whispers in the increasing murmur of the small crowd.

"There have been more wolf attacks on the border of the eastern village did you hear? Terrible tragedy."

And

"It ain't no natural thing, this. Strange for a wolf to hunt alone. Strange indeed."

Or

"You heard of the ancient moon curse and the moon bitten?"

At this, Blaxton swears and blasphemes to the Gods, and pulls me into him, protecting me from the worthless tittle-tattle. Even Woolsey and his friends look uncomfortable with the fever pitch of gossip beginning to babble and overflow like the brook in early spring. All except the girl, Kaya, by Woolsey's side. Kaya covers her smile with slender hand, and feigns a cough to cover her laughter. Woolsey whispers something in her ear though it's me he watches, and the smile slides from her face like melted candle wax.

With the gossip and the looks and the pain pulsating in my arm, I cannot help but show the scowl I've been hiding behind my composed facade. It is not that I expect respect from anyone, I just thought they would at least wait until I was out of earshot before they began their raving ramblings. And I can't help but feel my private promise—my vendetta—rising to the surface as yet more details of attacks are discussed behind cold, cupped hands.

"I'm going to kill this wolf," I involuntary call. Everyone looks as surprised by my outburst as I feel, but I cannot stop the anger pouring from my mouth. "I will hunt it, and kill it, if it's the last thing I do."

"Red," Blaxton urges me to stop. I have their attention now. Now they are not talking about me. Now, they are listening to me. I wriggle under his grip.

"I won't stop hunting it until I kill it dead, even if I have to rip the beast apart with my own teeth," I growl, shocked my by venom.

"*Red?*" Blaxton says, surprised this time. He widens his eyes, urging me to stop.

Several women cross themselves as their men pull them away, disgusted. Good. Having their disgust is better than having their pity. I shirk from Blaxton's hold.

"I need to be alone," I say. I need to mourn, I need to feel the pain and emptiness of my home without Grandma's body *keeping* inside as it has been. Blaxton nods, and kisses me once firmly on the forehead.

"At least let me walk you home?" he asks but I turn him down.

"The walk will clear my mind, and it's daylight. I have nothing to fear but the insidious gossip. Please," I say, and so he nods and reluctantly follows the funeral party away. Though he does turn his head over his shoulder to offer a weak smile. My own smile is too late arriving and so he misses it, lowering his head and shoulders like a scolded dog as he leaves. He knows when he is beaten, and I curse myself. He's the only thing I have left in the world and I'm pushing him away—pushing him away because I can't stand the thought of one more ounce of pain my future could hold if he is taken next.

I watch the small crowd disperse awhile. Their black funeral capes and gowns dot across the frigid, white landscape like a spreading disease. Gossip is muted now by winter's clutch and all I hear is the repetitive thud of frozen black soil pounding on Grandma's coffin as the grave diggers fill the hole in the ground but not the one in my heart.

I turn to go, pulling the red hood of my cape over my hair. I elected not to wear the traditional black garb of the grieving, despite the outrageous looks cast my way. Grandma had made the cape especially for me, so I can do with it what I wish. But somehow the red looks less vibrant now, the edges tinted with grief and darkness. I tell myself it is simply the damp seeping up the heavy hem from the sleety snow. But I'm not sure if I believe my own words. And I wonder if Grandma is pulling the colour from the cape, from my life, and into her grave, trying to replace her blood spilt on the rug at home.

A strong grip grasps my wrist, pulling me from my thoughts. I spin into Woolsey as he yanks me toward him, his face inches from my own. His warm, whitened breath touches my face and his delicious lips pull into a wolfish grin. I try not to notice his liquid gold eyes, his musky scent filling my lungs with a carnal craving.

"Be careful," he warns—threatens. "Be *very* careful."

I don't trust his perfect face, his honey smooth

words. I don't trust the way his body pulls me towards him like a magnet—our hips touching, our legs intertwined.

I try pulling away, but his grip is relentless. Like being caught within the jaws of a beast.

"Get off," I warn through clenched teeth, "You cannot have me." An echo from a past promise. Grandma's promise. I shudder.

He raises an eyebrow and looks around himself to check if we are alone. We are.

His hand reaches for my bandaged wound and he cocks his head to the side like an inquisitive hound.

"Does it hurt?" He asks as he wraps his fingers and palm around my arm. His touch is somehow as light as a butterfly landing upon the puncture wounds, but the pain raises a guttural scream that does not sound like my own.

And then everything turns to darkness.

INTERLUDE - DARKNESS

The wound pulls me into itself, and the world surrounding me evaporates into only this small space. The space blazing a blacker darkness through my veins. As before, pain floods my body with a shredding and tearing deeper than flesh; a severing of my soul, perhaps, if such a thing could occur. I clutch at it with my mind, gripping claws of desperate hopelessness. There is nothing else. Nothing but the pain and the small spaces in which to hide. And here, I find solace in my wound once more. I go inwards, I give up. I allow the darkness to become me.

6

I AM NOT sure how long I left my body, but when I return, I find myself back in Grandma's cottage. A fire roars in the hearth and dusk has settled outside. It casts a strange half-light through the window, a blue hue of twilight upon snow shimmering like an otherworldly land. I have no idea how I got here— did I walk in my dreamlike state, my subconscious guiding my body as I lost myself to the darkness?

My hair sticks to my face and the back of my neck, though I suspect the clamminess has nothing to do with the flames dancing gold and amber against the walls, but more to do with the rising infection pulsing in my arm.

I dare to remove the bandage for the first time. Slowly, I unravel the soiled, damp cloth, wincing as it reaches the site of the wound. It sticks, cloth to blood and pus leaking from the punctures. Grandma would have used a poultice, and I curse myself for not remembering sooner. I bite my lip and hold my breath as I get to the infected area, each unravel worse than the one before. The stench rises now, the stench of decay and rot, worse than the smell of Grandma before they took her away.

The final unravel is the worst, skin and the small hairs on my arms are caked with gore and they won't give up the cloth. I hold my breath and wince. Slowly and painfully, the bandage peels away, and it is all I can do not to retch at the sight of the wound.

The holes are deep and black, as depthless as the universe itself. Purple veins spread from each, outwards and upwards, connecting to those million tunnels through my skin. And these veins stretch further, grasping at clean white skin to pull into those black holes as if my entire body will vanish into them.

I should go to the doctor, I know I should. His homestead is not far away. But as I stare through the window, assaulted by a snow flurry edging its way to a blizzard, I wonder if it would be more prudent to wait until morning. As if taunting me, the wound grips my arm with its fang like pulse, a heat surges though my entire body making me dizzy. And I know…

This wound cannot wait.

If I leave it much longer, I may lose my arm altogether, my fingertips are already touched with a darkish hue. If I leave it completely, the infection could take over my entire body, and then I'll be lowered into the ground in a cheap wooden coffin just like Grandma.

Despite my hot flushes and clammy sweats, I don several layers of warmer clothes, noticing my cloak hanging on the back of the chair by the fire to dry. I can't remember putting it there, but who knows what I do when those painful dreams pull me into themselves. But as I grab at the thick fabric, I realise something is not right.

The hem of my red cape is still black as if wet, yet it is dry to the touch. I scrunch it in my fist to make doubly sure. And more disturbing, it is not only the hem. The blackness is spreading—just like the dark veins on my wound—greedy and wanting; stripping the colour away just as the wolf had drained Grandma's blood.

A lone howl echoes into the valley—a sound held steady by the white-capped land. The beast is not far away and I feel my hackles rise. Before I have time to change my mind, I fling my blackening cloak over my shoulders, fastening it tight against the snowy night. And just in case, as the lone wolf howls again, this time closer, I grab Grandma's gutting knife. She used it for gutting plump summer fish, just one clean slice would see their innards exposed.

It feels right in my hand. Heavy with responsibility.

I step out into the night.

7

THE WIND HAS PICKED UP. It howls its lonesome eerie tune, another layer to accompany the howls from the savage beast hiding in the wilds. Swirls of thick snow fling about the dense air in abstract patterns, and I make out the faces of Grandma and Blaxton much like the way I used to make out faces in the patterns of the now blood-stained rug when I was but a child—seeing things when they are not there.

I wonder if that is what I'm doing now when pondering the wolf's attacks. Are they the pure chance maul of a dumb and hungry beast, starving in the winter's barren embrace? Or are the attacks planned assaults and something far more sinister?

Perhaps the wolf, too, has a pattern. There is

certainly a pattern within which the beasts have killed my own family. Perhaps they've marked us as their prey, much the way a territorial and possessive wolf marks its territory. Trudging through the thick snow, my eyes all but closed against the blizzard whirling at my face, I wonder if I should find out more about the other attacks —discover other patterns with other families. Maybe I should track the beast and discover its wily ways and intent before killing it and its secrets dead...

...All this is superstitious nonsense. The curse, I know I'm thinking about the curse, but it is nothing but hearsay, the wild gossip of young children and bored housewives. But still... the morphing blooded footsteps in the snow. My hand instinctively reaches to protect the wound on my arm, and the tiring journey begins to dissolve my fanciful thoughts.

I shuffle along as best I can, my legs plunging into soft snow up to my knees. My breath is short and catches against my scarf leaving it hot and damp against my otherwise chilled face. And the world feels as though it has shrank to the small space within my cape—my inhales and exhales deafening, filling my ears and head like the *swooshing* of a rough and ragged shoreline. All my extremities

are numb—all but the wound, of course. The wound still pulses with flames and fire.

The thick blanket of white hides the well-worn path but I still recognise the route to the doctor's abode through the trees which meander this way and that. Though tonight, the empty branches bow towards me, ominous fingers of ice and frost grasping for life. No moon shines her light, she is late to rise, so I am at least a little thankful for the pale glow of the snow lighting the way.

A sense of vulnerability creeps along my skin. Hairs stand upright on the back of my neck and I look about myself. Someone, or *something*, is watching me. I feel the eyes devouring me in its gaze. My mouth dries and I quicken my pace, thankful for the glow of a warm fire emanating from the windows of doctor's home through the trees.

I breathe a sigh of relief and pick up my pace. Warmth and help are but a few yards away. Of course, the howl would come now, breaking though the shrieking blizzard when I am so close to sanctuary.

The low and resonate tune sings out into the night, holding for several long breaths and heart-beats. Is it a threat, or an invite? I hover, turning to

the doctor's warm glowing cabin, then back into the darkness of the forest's cavernous clutch—weighing my options.

But my hesitation has sealed my fate, stripping choice away. The paw prints are light and fast in the snow, galloping towards me, flicking snow around itself as it bounds. I hear the heavy breathing of the beast in full flight, the growl beneath its breath. Its eyes piercing through the blizzard. Primal fear races blood around my body—the fight or flight response of the hunted.

I grip the knife in my right hand and drop my body weight downward, an attack stance. No flight for me. And I wait, breath steady as the wolf launches through the air.

8

THE WOLF's body pounds into me. Air bursts from my lungs like a spewing volcano as we tumble into the ice-cold snow. It growls and snaps and yelps, a feverish attack echoing my grandma's death.

I scream at the wolf. Not the scream of fear, or a plea for help. No. I bellow my own battle cry, my own roar, my own howl. Any thoughts I had about discovering the lone wolf's secrets vanish. All I want is to kill this bastard that has already taken too much from me.

Anger and revenge have a primal power, an otherworldly strength that emanates now I as grapple the beast's body lurching on top of me and spin it onto its back in the snow. Grandma's gutting knife is clutched firmly in my hand, I plunge the blade into the side of the beast as it wrestles beneath me.

It yelps, but raged and ferocious, I continue—stab wound after stab wound. The wolf's hot blood warms my freezing cold hands and specs of its ailing life force spatters upon my face. It whimpers, but I don't stop.

Can't stop.

Screaming and plunging over and over again. Its blue eye, piercing against the snow stained red, begs, *pleads,* for mercy I do not have.

The beast stops fighting, stops defending itself but enraged, I continue. I continue until I feel faint with exertion. Plunging deeper into my own wrath. I continue until my sickening actions fill my body with nausea. Finally, breathless, I fall onto the crimson stained snow, weeping as the wolf takes its last few shallow breaths.

And it is done.

My hands tremble.

The bitter, terrible, disgusting revenge has been repaid. The vendetta accomplished. I retch, vomiting on all fours. And I can't help but wonder; is this the end? The end of a story where savage wild wolves take my family?

I stagger to my feet, attempting to wipe the

blood from my face with my sleeve, though I imagine it only serves to smear across my cheeks like a victorious hunter. I don't know if the wolf still breathes, I don't know for sure if it is yet quite dead, but regardless, there is no life to live within its decimated shell of a body. Its pale blue eye stares up at me, empty and unseeing. And I stare back, noticing the weight of the knife in my hand. It has become more. It feels heavier, a burden I did not expect. It carries my curse, my revenge, and my hateful attack that still sickens my bones.

One-by-one, my fingers unfurl from the hilt, and the bloodstained blade falls, its tip penetrating into the soft red snow beside my feet.

Closure. The end of the old. New beginnings. With one last bite of venom, I kick the beast in the guts, it does not react. Then, backing away with unsteady steps, blood drunk, I stumble towards the safety of the doctor's cabin.

9

I DON'T EVEN KNOCK. I half barge and half fall into the doctor's house, collapsing on the threshold.

"What the…?" Doctor Revel cries. There is a thump of a book on the ground and the clattering of something wooden—a stool or a chair perhaps, I cannot look up to ascertain. I just lay with my blood-smeared face upon the soft rug, hoping it does not stain like my own. The smells of family life lull my thoughts away; the sweetness of fresh bread baking, the musk of smoke and wood smouldering in the open hearth. Fresh sheets must be drying somewhere by the sweet perfumed fragrance enveloping me in a motherly embrace.

"Dear Lord," the doctor cries. "Renee, fetch some blankets, the child is freezing to death."

The doctor holds my limp wrist in his fingers, feeling for my pulse. But all I want to do is close my eyes to forget the blinding pain and biting cold… the terrible flashes of nightmarish images replaying in my mind.

Within moments, a soft, heavy warmth covers my body and a wet flannel wipes clean my hands, though not my soul.

"Don't worry about the blood on her hands," Doctor Revel says to his wife. He flips me onto my back and the world lurches within my stomach. With firm fingers, he opens one of my eyes, then the other. But I fail to see anything except the flash of fur and fang dancing on the canvas of my mind.

"Quickly," he says from somewhere far away. "It's Scarlet's granddaughter. Looks like another wolf attack. Help me carry her to the fire, she's a bloody deadweight."

Hands grapple my wrists and ankles and I feel the world move, then a delightful warmth and crackle as I am set down. The doctor begins tearing at my clothes, his hands running along my body. I cannot protest, for I cannot move.

"Where's the wound?" Renee's soft voice tinkles and there is an unnerving and wanting silence even to my half-addled mind. "All this blood, there must be a wound."

More tearing of clothes, more feeling of hands. More time and space and yet still I cannot rouse myself to say the words I must.

"I still cannot find the injury," Doctor Revel says, his hands still searching my body.

"Perhaps she found someone else attacked? Perhaps she tried to save them like she did her grandma?" suggests the tinkling voice. "We should go out, see who's out there, perhaps she came only to relay a message?"

"Out there? With the wolf at large once more?"

I can't let them leave me here, not without finding the festering wound on my arm. I have already lost so much, I do not want to lose my arm as well, or worse. Perhaps it's the noose of death gripping the edges of my subconscious and the windpipe within my throat, but my eyes fling open.

"Red!" Doctor Revel calls in his deep resonate voice. "Thank the heavens. What happened, who's injured?"

"My arm," I croak. My voice sounds weird, tinny and not my own. The doctor picks up my left arm. "No," I say, "the other."

Another long, heavy pause. My gaze begins to

focus. I see the worried stare between husband and wife, their silent fears as they look at my arm and to each other once more.

"That bad?" I ask trying to sound a little light or hopeful, but sound neither.

"Red?" The doctor asks. His voice solid and professional. He is not talking to me as a long time family friend anymore. "Red, what happened… out there?"

"My arm!" I scream, cursing their concern for the dead wolf. "Tell me, how bad is it!"

But he doesn't tell me, instead he places his hand on my clammy forehead. "She has a fever," he says to his wife, then to me, "is anyone else injured?"

He speaks slowly, as if I am a child that might not understand his simple words. I gather just enough strength to sit up, though it takes every ounce I have. Grappling my arm, I shove the wound, oozing black blood, to his face. "Tell me, *please*? Will it kill me?"

"Will what kill you?"

"The wound!" I scream.

"There *is* no wound." The doctor's eyebrows scrunch together—his forehead a ploughed and furrowed field of lost hope.

My mouth drops open as I stare at him, then my septic wound, and back to him again. I hear his words but am unable to process what he's saying, unable to process my own thoughts.

"It could be the fever," he whispers to his wife. "The fever can cause hallucinations. Or perhaps it's something else, some way to deal with the internal pain of losing Scarlet to the wolves like her mother before."

"I'm… I'm not hallucinating…" I say but am unsure if the words leave my lips or simply circulate in my mind.

"But that does not explain the blood," Renee says, and I can't tell if her whispering is quieter still or if I'm slipping away from the world.

I claw at consciousness, grasp it tight. "What about *my* blood, my *black* blood!" I scream and this time they both look at me. My wound blisters with searing pain. "It's right there between your fingers."

The doctor shakes his head and with an all too mournful face, says, "The girl is losing her mind."

Then their words are just mumbles and muffles as I fade into a place that does not exist.

INTERLUDE - EVERYTHING

Fangs, flesh, rotting blood. Claws, fur, moon. Images flicker and morph, a continual dream of doom with no sense or meaning.

You can't have her.

You can't have her.

You can't have her.

Grandma's voice. Grandma's call. Swirling in my head filled with fragments of moments past.

Blades, wounds, fading life. Consciousness, madness, a blood-dripped knife. Trees enclosing. Moon bearing down. A howl. A promise. A change.

She's losing her mind.

On repeat. Over and over and over and over and over and over and over and over... Has my mind already gone? Gone where? Where am I? Who am I?

Four holes in my arm, calling me home.

Be quiet. Be still. Rest in this place.

No. *You can't have her.*

Tick tock tick tock.

My grandmother's clock stares at me—its face a full moon. Its pendulum a swaying knife dripping with blood. I'm losing sense of time, rhyme, life.

I fight it. I fight this venom in my blood and claw my way out of the dream…

10

I WAKE WITH A START, jolting upright on the too soft bed. Sunbeams force their way through the window shutters—golden lines of light gilding all it touches within the dim shadows.

"Red? Oh, thank God." Blaxton all but pins me back to the bed with his embrace. His scent is intoxicating and confusing and I don't know where I am.

Feeling my unease, he collects himself, his ruggedly handsome face pale and gaunt with worry. He rests a hand on my forehead and he smiles. Despite myself, I cannot help but smile back and for one sweet moment, none of this has happened. Grandma. The funeral. The killing of the beast. And yet...

"I did it," I say, triumphant. "I killed the wolf that mauled Grandma."

His smile fades and another look takes over his features. What is it? Pain? Sadness? *Pity?*

The door bursts open and Doctor Revel blusters through the doorway.

"Thank the heavens. You're awake." His face is red from the cold, his breath short. His hands, although clean, still has traces of blood sticking to the cuticles around his bitten down nails. He looks at me in the way only a doctor can, and gulps. "Are you, *well?*"

"Thirsty," I say and the doctor nods.

"Of course. I'll fetch you water. Blaxton, perhaps you will assist me?"

Blaxton frowns at the doctor then smiles at me apologetically. His thick lips now pulled into a tight line. He rises and follows the doctor from the room, though he clings to my hand with an outstretched arm until only our fingers intertwine, finger tips, then I feel nothing but space.

A space and a private peace. The beast is dead, and I killed it.

Looking down at a clean night slip I'm wearing, I realise someone has washed the blood from my body and I can't help but wonder who. The thought of Blaxton seeing my naked skin beneath my clothes both thrills and terrifies me, the idea of his hands trailing the contours of my waist, my hips, my... I calm myself with the realisation the deed was probably carried out by Renee, the doctor's wife and any thoughts of passion are dampened.

The wounds on my arm are clean, and without the oozing blood and puss obscuring my view, I can see their depths more clearly. They are no longer mere puncture wounds the size of a wolf's malicious fangs, but seem to emulate four moon phases of the blackened eclipse. And the veins, or *vines*, connecting them, dance in intricate patterns. A delicate dance of shooting stars and expansion. I can't help but stare. Stare deep down into those holes. Losing myself in another universe.

Falling.

Compelled.

Tick tock.

A cluttering of a bowl in the kitchen breaks the strange hold on me, and I shake my head, woozy, before checking if my strange compulsion has been witnessed. It has not, but it has reminded me of the doctor's last words before I fell out of consciousness.

There is no wound... The fever could be causing hallucinations.

But I have no fever now, and yet the mark is still here as clear as day.

There is the mumble of hushed conversation in the next room. I recognise Blaxton's tone and I strain to hear the words they wish to hide from me.

"Grief is a powerful emotion, so too the denial of it," says the doctor. "It can push people to the edge of their emotional limits—make them do things they would otherwise never consider. Tread lightly, for the worst thing one can do with a patient fraying on the edges of madness is to confront them with their own fantasies."

"You don't think she…" Blaxton trails off and there is an awkward silence.

"I think we need to be on our guard. Allow her to talk with you, believe—allow her to *think* you believe in her tales, hallucinations, anything else that might somehow give us clues to her real mental state and capacity."

"I will not deceive her," Blaxton says, his voice louder now, a sharp edge to its tone.

"No, no." The doctor's voice placating. "Merely for her own benefit, allow her to open up to you.

We need to get to the bottom of this before any further action is taken."

Blaxton starts to speak but his words are cut off by a crashing door and a roaring call.

Woolsey. I can hear that rich tenor to his silken smooth voice despite his bitter tones. "It happened last night, so I am told. Why did no one alert me of this massacre sooner?"

"Please, Master Frey," the doctor hushes. "Please, this is a delicate matter and Red is in a delicate state."

Delicate? If there is one way I do not want Woolsey and his hungry eyes to think of me, it's delicate.

"Red?" Woolsey says. "What is she doing here? What has she to do with this blood bath?"

I rise, and tip toe between shadow and light as the sunbeams continue to push their way through the shutters of the darkened room. I peep through the gap in the door, and some relentless force pulls me forward.

"I have everything to do with the blood bath. It was me," I say through clenched teeth as I tramp into the room. The front door is still open and the low setting sun blazes on the snow outside. In the distance I see the bulk of the dead surrounded by stains of crimson and revenge. "It was me, last night. I killed the wolf who attacked Grandma—the wolf who attacked me."

The doctor crosses himself and takes a step away. Woolsey and Blaxton stare at one another. No one speaks. I shuffle on the spot, suddenly aware I am dressed only in a nearly translucent white night shift. It is the doctor's wife Renee who fills the heavy silence.

"It was not a wolf we are talking about, Red," she begins. Her face is pale and drawn. Her hands are shaking. "Kaya, her body was found just yards from the here—"

Kaya, the girl who feigned and fawned over Woolsey at Grandma's funeral.

"—The wolf killed Kaya? How? *When?*" I ask, amazed that the beast could have resurrected itself from my attack, and I begin to wonder, again, about superstitious gossip and full moon curses.

Woolsey bites his lip. Blaxton runs his hands through his thick blonde hair and turns his face from me. The doctor slumps in his chair making dust particles explode upwards to dance in a stray sunbeam.

Renee takes one minuscule step toward me. Her hands are held in a strange way at her sides, as if any moment she may turn and take flight. "Kaya was not attacked by a wolf, Red. She was killed —murdered."

Murdered.

Tick tock.

Fangs and flesh and rotting blood.

"Murdered?" I repeat, replaying last night's attack in my mind. The one blue eyes staring up at me in the snow.

"Yes. And the murderer left their knife next to her body…"

And the murderer left their knife…

"What about the wolf's body? Where did you find that?" Perhaps it's the wrong question when a young girl has been found dead, but I can't think straight, my mind, it shatters. Renee shakes her head a sure 'no'. Fragments of memory and imagination spread outwards into the universe. "But I killed the wolf. I killed the wolf just there!" I cry, if only to remind myself of what really happened. I point outside to a lifeless bulk in the distance, surrounded by crimson stained snow. They all follow the line of my finger. Nobody looks back.

"That's Kaya's body," Blaxton says but he looks directly at Woolsey, whose eyes shift, uneasy. "There was no wolf found."

There was no wolf found.

There is no wound.

But there is a knife.

And I know I left it in the snow next to the fur-covered body.

11

A LOADED SILENCE. The ticking of time stops, hovers. The world holds its breath.

Outside, a dark cloud tracks over the sun, devouring the morning light and replacing it with shadows. Shadows of doubt. Shadows of suspicion. The gloom creeps along the snow from the open door, consuming the once glinting light. Its shadow prowls over the threshold, moving along the floorboards towards the tip of my toes. I cannot bear to look at the faces I know are staring at me.

"Red?" Doctor Revel asks quietly, as if I were a wild animal that may attack at any moment. "I need to ask you something…" He hesitates for so long I am forced to look at him, to read his face, his terrified and horrified face. "Are you *quite* sure a *wolf* killed your grandmother?"

His words, his accusation slams into my chest, gripping my bruised and assaulted heart. I stagger backwards as the unspoken words spell themselves out in the chilling air.

"You think I made it up? You think I murdered my—"

"Doctor!" Blaxton yells, cutting me off. In three rushed strides, he is at my side. "You can't possibly be accusing her of…"

An unspeakable accusation.

Blaxton pulls me to him, wrapping me entirely into his protective embrace. The doctor raises one eyebrow and turns to the crimson-stained snow outside. To the bulk of a dead body and my knife.

Woolsey glares, his nostrils flare. He says not a word but his venom is palpable even from the other side of the room, splitting through the gaps between Blaxton and myself; penetrating, menacing, but nowhere as near as dangerous as my own thoughts.

Was it a wolf I killed last night?
Was it a wolf that killed Grandma?
There is no wound.
She is losing her mind.
Grief.

anger and threats. And I remember his own threat to me 'Be careful, be very careful.' What does he know that he refuses to say?

"Red, please," Blaxton says softly, but his face is stern. He opens his arms, gesturing for me to return to his safety. Does he too sense the threats behind his friend's hostile eyes? Can he feel the danger?

Be very careful.

Woolsey grips my arms to push me away, his fingers brush against the phases of the moon wound. As he does, I scream out and we both stagger backwards as if electrified. *Now* he looks at me, wild eyed. I don't know what happened but I'm breathless and heady and feint. Does he feel it too?

"Get away from her," Blaxton yells.

Lightning strikes the cabin, a crackling welt as a storm descends. A roar of thunder rips across the canvas of the greying sky. The ground shudders. Outside, a wolf howls and we all turn to the open door, following the sound.

A pack of wolves, six, perhaps seven or more, trot to the bulk of the dead body under the darkening shadow of storm clouds. They sniff the red snow, one wolf pushes the body with its snout. *Kaya's body.* For one terrified moment, I am convinced the beasts will start feasting on the dead girl. My innards tighten in response. But they don't feast. They howl, a chorus of mourning and sadness echoes in the air. And the largest wolf, perhaps the pack leader, picks Kaya up in its mouth as if a young pup and carries her away into the woods, her arms and legs trailing the ground.

"My goodness," Renee says, her tiny bird like hand to her unhinged jaw. "They're taking her body to the den to feed the pack." She gags and runs to the bathroom.

Woolsey watches Blaxton, then he turns to me, then outside. "I can't stay here," he says, giving me a disdainful glare. "Kaya's brothers deserve an explanation," he says before sprinting out into the wilderness.

Does he know something I do not? Is he not somehow connected to all of this?

Think

Think

Think

Blooded paw prints morphing from Grandma's cabin to Blaxton's homestead. Woolsey turning up when the wolves attacked Blaxton's horse. He turns up now when I attacked a wolf. He's seen my wound no matter his denial. His warning. His hungry, hungry liquid-gold eyes. I start to sweat but words and thoughts and meaning swim around my head.

He knows something.

He knows something.

He knows something.

Tick tock tick tock.

The phases of the moon expanding.

Fur and fang.

"Red?" Blaxton shouts, urgent. I hear him but I can't shake my thoughts. I can't stop the rocking in my mind.

He knows something.

"Red?" He calls again. "Doctor, what is wrong with her? Do something."

And my hands are restrained, but I don't fight it. I'm far away.

I'm somewhere else.

I'm someone else.

Falling…

THERE IS ONLY one thing I need, and that is the answer to my question;

Am I *really* losing my mind?

I feel a rope wrap around my wrists.

"Doctor, I don't think you need to—" Blaxton is cut off.

"—The girl is clearly not in her right mind. We need to restrain her so I can administer the sedation —she has already killed that poor innocent child under her delusions, perhaps her own kin too."

"She would never have killed her grandmother," Blaxton spits, but I wonder, *would I? Wouldn't I?* Wasn't she the only person stopping Blaxton and I from being together?

Fangs and flesh, the taste of blood splattered on my lips.

I think back to the attack at my house. The wolf was already there, wasn't it? I heard it howl.

Or did the howling come from within.

I'm falling deep into my thoughts.

"The girl is catatonic. Quick, Renee, the tranquilliser," calls Doctor Revel. He has to call twice and somewhere in the back of my logical mind, I assume it is because Renee is still throwing up her breakfast in the toilet. There is shuffling and shouting and arguing and I can only think of the bloody paw prints morphing in the snow.

The trembling starts, a fear, a terror.

"No. No. No. No," I begin, faster and faster until the words are connected and only one—like the images in my head.

The footprints—were they… *mine?*

"It's okay, Red, it's okay," the doctor soothes. "This won't hurt but it will help calm your nerves."

"Doctor, are you sure this is necessary?" Blaxton asks.

But *I* am not sure. I'm not sure at all. Not sure of anything or anyone… except Woolsey.

He saw the wound.

He grabbed at it after the funeral making me pass out.

If he saw the wound then none of this, none of

these so-called delusions are false. All I need to do is find a way to make everyone else believe me.

"You'll just feel a small scratch,' Doctor Revel says.

Blaxton holds me upright, stopping me from falling to my knees.

Renee looks on, her fingers covering her open mouth.

"No!" I roar this time. "Get off me, get off me. I can prove it. I can prove everything if you just let me go."

I wriggle and writhe but the men's hold is strong.

"Please, Red," Blaxton begs. "Why are you doing this?"

"You cannot reason with her, she is not in her right mind," the doctor says, breathless, his grip tightening as I try to lose his hold. "The mad of mind are prone to violence when their delusions are called out. I'll tell you more when she—" he grunts as I stamp on his foot and smash my head backwards into his nose. I hear a soft crack of cartilage as he swears. "Hold still, you bloody savage."

I feel a power from within, like the cosmic universe sparkling from my wound around my body. If I let the doctor convince Blaxton I am mad, then what hope do I have? I *have* to get the evidence. I *have* to find some truth. I burst free like a comet.

"Let me go!" I scream, wide-eyed and breathless. And I can only imagine how I look in their eyes —my night slip wet and translucent with sweat. My hair wild and stuck to my clammy forehead. My desperate eyes darting from memory to imaginations and back to the people in the room, searching for even a hint of belief from their astonished eyes. All the while, they stare back, wearing their doubtful and fearful thoughts on their faces.

And like some wild and untamed beast, I turn and run barefoot, yet determined, into the wilderness and the brewing storm outside.

I HAVE TO FIND WOOLSEY. I have to make him tell me all he knows. I have to prove I am not some wild monster, a killer. A murderer. A mad woman. Yet galloping through the storm away from the safety of the doctor's cabin, I realise I am at least one version of crazy. I know running barefoot and bare-legged knee deep in snow, wearing only a shift is madness. And surely, my awareness of that means I can't be completely insane. Though it *is* insane to keep going.

But keep going I will.

The strange storm brings snowflakes as big as overripe apples to blizzard this way and that, obscuring my sight as I run. Though they do not obscure the bloody patch left by the wolf or Kaya, depending on what side of madness my mind rests.

I stop, my bare feet in the crimson stain slowly disappearing—like my sanity—with the covering of fresh snow. No, not a covering, but a concealing. A concealing of truth and I feel my own mind doing the very same thing. Concealing things of which it does not want to see or remember.

The blackouts.

There is no telling from the shape left on the ground if this was girl or beast I killed. Blood is blood, no matter from where it comes. But it *is* my knife. The pewter hilt dim in the overcast light.

I bend to retrieve it.

To conceal the evidence.

More snow falls.

If only Woolsey would admit to what he saw— my wound, his warning.

I reach the woods and their barren branches, making my way to the higher ground where magnificent firs call to me. Like some primal instinct I run like a wild thing, seeking protection from the coldness of land and thoughts. I cannot go home. I cannot bear to see what I fear I might. Fractured memories—different to the ones already in my mind.

And I have a feeling, an urge, a sense I might find Woolsey here.

I stumble to a halt, gasping and grasping at my heaving chest with hands that tremble with sudden realisation.

Woolsey did not see my wound.

He saw my bandage.

My heart sinks to the frigid white ground, and my body follows as I collapse to my knees. My breath catches and rasps at the back of my dry throat as I stare at my arm. The wounds—the marks, they are pale and gaunt, as if they are sinking into my skin. Sinking into my soul.

They are hardly there at all.

And I can't help but wonder what happens during my blackouts. Are these fractured moments memories or ideas of memories? Do I imagine what happens in my mind as I create an entirely different reality?

Am I… am I a *monster*? A *murderer*?

I howl. I howl in the relentless snow falling from darkened thunderclouds, watching as lightning crackles across the sky, illuminating the black clouds with gold. Rumbles near and far charge across the land.

I don't know who I am.

Another growl stops my sinister thoughts. And another. Another. And another. A pack of amber eyes coalesce through the thick blizzard. Yapping and spitting between bared teeth as the wolves circle close. I'm surrounded. They stalk ever closer. I squeeze my eyes shut and open them again. This isn't a dream, is it? This isn't another blackout? These aren't just my thoughts stalking me? Or are they?

I clamber to my feet with movements so slow I barely seem to move at all.

My heart pounds.

This is all in my head. This is all in my head. This is all in my head.

But still, the beasts encroach.

Yapping, snapping, snarling. They keep coming. My thoughts or monsters, I cannot tell which.

A flash of white fur to my right, swift as lightning. Loud as thunder as it growls and roars and yelps.

A white wolf. *The white wolf?*

A memory flickers; bared teeth crunching down on bone and sinew.

Eyes wide, I have nowhere to go. The beast has me in its sights, again, and it's galloping towards me with impossible speed. Snow flickers up from its paws, saliva spits from its mouth. The surrounding wolves draw ever closer, my world ever smaller.

If I am mad, none of this matters.

If I am not, then I am as good as dead.

The majestic white wolf launches through the air, over the circling wolves, pounding into my body.

I scream as we tumble. The world spins, faster and faster as we plunge down the hill. Out of control in a fall that would have killed us both if not for the snow-laden slope. Pounding bodies and white fur and flesh. The paws grip me as we continue our plunge. The beast is no longer snarling. Instead, our faces lock as we plummet. It's golden eyes, hungry. I've seen this look before. And nothing else matters now as the white world blurs.

In my right hand, Grandma's gutting knife. My fingers close around the handle tight. But my mind pauses.

What if this is not a wolf?

What if this is another, saving me from the beasts within my mind, saving me from my beastly thoughts? What if, in attempting to save myself from this fate—these thoughts—I kill again?

But I feel the wolf's musky breath on my face. Its fur in my clutches. My wound tingles beneath my skin. The knife feels ready. Surely this cannot be all in my mind? The fear grows. Survival instinct kicks in. The white wolf stares.

I roar, and plunge the knife into its side.

14

IT HOWLS, short and sharp. Eyes staring into mine, the beast's face, its fur, its *shape* is changing. Morphing. Reforming.

I pull the knife from its side, and the blade sucks as if not wanting to let go of flesh. Warm blood trickles down the blade to cover my fingertips. I unfurl my fingers; the blade slips from my grip and I fear I have killed another as I did poor Kaya.

The tumbling ceases with an abrupt thud as my back crashes into the plateau. I let out a groan, and although we are both motionless, the world still somehow spins on its axis. I can barely breathe, as if a single sound will break this spell. His face is so close to mine I can smell his spicy breath hot against my own. His hungry honey-amber eyes bore into my soul. He's trembling, the entire weight of his quivering body warm against my own. I no longer feel fur in my hands but warm, soft skin.

Did I ever feel the fur?

"Are you okay?" Woolsey asks.

My eyes widen. "Am *I* okay?" I ask, incredulous. "I just stabbed you and you're asking if I'm okay?"

My heart pounds on the verge of breaking. My mind swirls. I can barely breathe with the mass of confusion and craziness.

"Shhh," Woolsey whispers. "I'm okay, I promise, look."

With his warm hand atop of mine, he guides my touch across the contours of his lean, muscular body, and although covered in warm blood, there is no wound. I grasp at his exposed torso, feeling for something I know is not there—it reminds me of may own wound.

"Shhh," he whispers again. He takes exaggerated slow breaths, encouraging me with a nod to do the same.

I watch his perfect lips move but cannot speak. Instead, I copy his breathing, trying to make sense of the insensible world playing in my mind. His arms are wrapped around me, and mine around him, where I once clutched white fur. Snow has caught on his long black eyelashes, a flush of red raised to his cheeks. He trails his fingers gently down my face, fingertips burning against my skin. They stop, and trace the contour of my lips, that I open, hungrily.

He leans into me, I feel his lips brush against my own and I can't fight the opposing desires from within. Breathless, I raise my hips and my lips to his own and...

The curdling of Grandma's blood stuck in her ravaged throat as she dies.

The ice white fur of the attacking wolf. Hungry, amber eyes.

The pieces of the puzzle begin to fit together.

"You?" I growl. "It was you who killed Grandma, you bastard."

My hand fumbles in the snow as I grapple for the knife once more. It takes only half a breath to find it and plunge it into his body.

He yelps, grabbing my hand on the knife and pulling it out of his sliced skin. He snarls, and morphs, and growls, changing back into a wolf. And as he does, I watch the wound. I watch how it closes as his body changes. Watch how the skin knits together with the metamorphosis.

And it makes sense.

That's why Woolsey had no wound after I stabbed him when attacking Grandma.

They don't take their wounds with them when they change.

I think of Kaya. She *was* a wolf, no matter what the doctor believes. I can only assume I just didn't give her the time to morph into a healthy new skin with my frenzied attack. And at this point, I don't know if this fact makes me sad or glad.

But Woolsey.

I now know his secrets. His warnings. His appearances at strange time and places. He *did* know about my wound, regardless of the bandage. He knew because he made it.

"I'll kill you, you bastard, if it's the last thing I do."

But he turns and gallops away into the firs and snow.

I think back to the gun used to put Blaxton's poor horse out of her misery—by a wolf attack probably carried out by Woolsey himself.

Another fear creeps into my mind as I relive the

animosity between Blaxton and Woolsey at Doctor Revel's cabin. The loaded looks. The heavier silence. And I don't know which I need more; to warn Blaxton of Woolsey's wolfish ways, or to grab Blaxton's gun and kill the beast myself.

15

BY THE TIME I reach the pathway to Blaxton's cabin, all my fight has gone.

My legs burn with fatigue, my body convulses with a coldness seeping deeper into my bones, and my lungs rasp in retaliation of the icy air. Though I am thankful the storm has ceased, the storm within still rages—all jagged edges grating upon my soul. I'm just too exhausted to allow it to surface.

I clamber up the steps to his veranda, almost on hands and knees, and push at the door with what little strength I have left in my body. The door swings open with a squeal, the innards of his dwelling blue and cold in the hostile light.

"Blaxton?" I call, my voice weak. "Blaxton?"

Everything goes black.

I MUST HAVE FALLEN ASLEEP—A beautiful dreamless sleep, for Blaxton has set me down by the empty hearth, smoothing my hair.

"You're freezing, my love." He pulls off his wolf-skin jacket and places it over me, tucking it around my body so the fur tickles my chin.

It feels warm. It feels right.

"I'll get the fire going…" his voice trails off and I can hear the concern in his unspoken words.

My teeth chatter too much to reply, and so instead, I take pleasure in watching him begin the simple ritual of fire starting. A pile of dried leaves. A selection of brittle twigs and kindling. Small logs that will light easily. Flint and steel.

In moments, there is a crackle and smoke smoulders from the leaves, wafting with the aroma of pine and forest. A small amber light glows, getting bigger as each flame touches another. And I stare at Blaxton now, knowing this is how our love developed. A small flicker, growing with each touch, each kiss of burning passion. And yet, the flames have not engulfed us entirely—not yet. For I have been smothering the final flame. Saving my virtue.

Wait for marriage. Passion will kill you. Love will keep you alive, that's what Grandma used to say. And I wonder whose love kept her alive, and whose love killed her. I know nothing of my grandfather, or *my* father for that matter. I have no real knowledge of men at all other than they have only become alluring this past summer. One more than any other. But I do know one thing—Grandma needed no love from a man to keep her alive, and in some ways, I think she wished the same for me.

But I am not her, nor my mother. And now, more than ever, I need to feel the touch of a true flame to sate the burning wilderness that has become my thoughts.

Blaxton's eyes squint as he watches me, and he holds his breath as if he is building up the courage to speak to me or waiting for me to speak to him; to give him answers, because the last time he saw me, I ran away like a wild thing into the storm alone. And now, I realise with sudden clarity, I have returned, covered in blood.

Again.

It's my turn to hold my breath, imagining how this must look to him.

Does he truly believe I have lost my senses?

I want to look at my wound but I am too scared to draw attention to it. I want to tell him about Woolsey but I'm suddenly too worried about what he may say. How can he believe me? How can *anyone* believe me?

I need a distraction, a reaction, to stop the crazy thoughts and imaginings for one fraction of a moment.

Blaxton excuses himself and when he returns with bundles of blankets in his hold, I am staring at my arm.

There is no wound, I hear the doctor say, yet, it *is* there, glimmering beneath the surface of my skin.

Four Full Moons.

Blaxton drops the blankets in a heap on the ground and sits with me, taking my arm in his hand. He kisses my fingers, my palm. His lips trail the soft underside of my arm from wrist to elbow where pale and unexposed skin sings at his touch. And he kisses what was once my wound. Each place the wolf's fangs pierced. I squirm with unease. *Exactly* where the wounds were.

Blaxton stops, aware of my sudden tenseness. "Shhh, Red. They have gone."

Yes, they have gone. Disappeared, sunk into my skin. Wait. "*What* has gone?" I quiz him.

How would he know? I thought he had not seen the wounds. I thought they were only in my imagination and…

"The hallucinations," he says softly, his lips tracing a line to my shoulders, his breath hot now against my neck.

I try to forget my swirling thoughts and my need to hang onto my memories, whether real or not. They *felt* real and I can't stop wondering what this means for me.

Let them go.

They have gone.

I clench my jaw. Yes, the hallucinations have gone, for now. The wounds have gone. Grandma and Kaya too. What happens when another blackout occurs?

I shudder. But this time with bliss.

Blaxton's hands grasp at my thighs, my hips, hands tracing forbidden lines beneath my white night shift towards my heart. I am cold no more, but I *am* breathless.

His tender hands turn into a strong embrace, pulling my body into him. And I allow him, melting into his skin. My fingers grasp at his sandy blond hair and we soften to the ground, the soft blankets surrounding us. He stops and stares at me, looking past my eyes and into my soul. A soundless ask for permission and, biting my lip, I nod.

Yes, I want this. I want you.

Without taking his honey eyes from my own, he pulls the slip up over my body, inch by inch. Each glimpse of skin revealed is a delicate and terrifying exposure.

"Are you sure?" he asks, breathless. Eyes wide, wandering over my body, he tries his hardest to keep eye contact, then shakes his head. Blaxton moves towards me, cupping my face in his hands. "You are beautiful," he whispers. And in this moment, I believe him. And I want nothing else but him and I together. "I want to make you mine."

You can't have her.

It whispers in my mind and I want Grandma to shut up and leave me alone. Leave me alone and in peace for this one perfect moment.

I pull at Blaxton's homespun top, ripping it over his shoulders and head as he lays me down, his body atop mine. His skin is soft and warm and the fire crackles, flames stronger and hotter now. I feel like we, too, are flames—dancing with one another.

Becoming one another as he parts my thighs that quiver with nervous excitement.

"Are you sure you are ready?" he asks.

And I am.

I am.

I am.

I feel him and pull him towards me, deeper, running my hands down his back.

I freeze.

"Do you want me to stop?" Blaxton asks, pausing.

And I say nothing, I just stare wide-eyed as a millions thoughts and ideas flash through my mind.

Tentatively, I run my hands down his back once more, feeling for the shape, the curve—the question. And though I have not *felt* this before, I have seen the shape of this mark. I will never forget it.

No!

This can't be... another hallucination?

I squirm away from him, panicked.

"Red?" he asks, concerned. I grab at the night slip and pull it over my exposed body, scrambling to my feet.

He grabs his shirt from the ground.

"No!" I scream, ripping it from his hands. "No, let me see."

I run around him yet he follows me, circling on the spot, a daze of confusion clouding his face.

"Let me see," I scream again.

The door pounds open and he turns.

I see it.

And I see Woolsey, storming through the door with murder on his face.

"I WARNED YOU TO BE CAREFUL!" Woolsey yells at me.

I try to back away. Why won't my legs move? Why can't the words explode from my mouth as he charges toward me? No, not to me, to Blaxton.

My wound pulses, itches, expands, shooting stars spreading along my skin, rippling, morphing changing.

"The doctor, his wife?" Woolsey glares at Blaxton. "Mauled to death. You, I assume. It's always been you, hasn't it?"

"I had to do something to stop Red getting incriminated by killing your mate—"

"—Kaya was not my *mate.*" Woolsey shoots a

greedy look at me. Blaxton follows his gaze and laughs.

"You're too late," Blaxton says, a smug tone full of pride. He looks at me and licks his lips.

A wolfish grin as he sees me frozen to the spot. A smile that says, *you're mine.*

You can't have her, I hear Grandma's last promise.

When Blaxton turns again, I see the mark fully —the black curve that follows the length of his spine like a question mark.

But I have questions no longer.

The white wolf. The black mark along its back as it ran yelping from Grandma's murder.

It was the key piece of evidence I had forgotten with the power of blooded morphed footprints, dead horses, knife blades and secrets.

The two men stand, tense and coiled, regarding each other.

"You claimed her then?" Woolsey says, full of spite.

Words crash in my mind but stay dammed behind my frozen tongue.

Blaxton smirks and nods. Where is the soft, gentle lover now? He swaggers towards me—the wolf who got the cream—and rests an arm around my shoulder. I can do nothing to push him away as a pulling sensation tugs at my soul, pulling me into the moon marks that suddenly glow blue and golden like the full moon slowly rising in the sky outside the window.

Woolsey shakes his head, disgust on his face.

"You cannot keep your place as leader of the pack after this abomination. There is already talk of a revolt. I had my suspicions and I will not hold the facts back. We are forbidden to bond with humans. We are not meant to *turn* them," Woolsey snarls.

Blaxton barks a laugh. "I can do what I want, just as my father did, and his before that."

"Well, congratulations. You did what they could not. Your grandfather failed when Scarlett killed him. Your father failed when Red's mother took her own life rather than turn." He pauses, watching me.

I feel a clawing at my fingers and toes, something desperate to escape my body.

The pain. The pressure. I scream at last but the sound echoes as a howl and I think I already know the truth.

Claws rip through my fingertips.

"What makes you think Red will ever forgive you for what you have done?" Woolsey shakes his head.

"Because we've mated, and so the bond has been made."

Woolsey hisses with clenched fists and turns away, while Blaxton looks to the window. A smile, a sickening smile that I cannot believe he can wear on his perfect face pulls his lips apart like a bloody slash. And yet, a pulling, an animal magnetism towards him that I can't shake.

He killed Grandma, allowed me to believe I was going crazy.

But the pull, stronger now, like lust and love and blood. I want to fight it, but cannot.

"When the full moon reaches the highest point, her metamorphosis will be complete. And there will be nothing she won't do for me. She was moon bitten by me, I am *inside* her—" Blaxton moves behind me, pulls my body into an embrace. His hands trail a line from my breasts to my stomach—lower still, and his breath shortens. "—I am inside her blood and sinew. And she will be mine. Forever. No matter what her dead and buried grandmother said."

You can never have her.

I want to scream but my mind and body rip apart, pulling away from each other. Pulling away to allow the monster from within to emerge. I feel it.

Fang and fur. Blood and lust. I revere the feel of his hard body against my own, but my soul revolts. My eyes beg Woolsey to help, but he looks on, helpless, all puppy-dog eyed. There is a hierarchy; I feel it now, instinctively. I feel Woolsey's submission—*my own*. Blaxton's dominance overpowering. Overbearing. Exquisite and beautiful.

I am his.

I rage against the feeling as I feel the pressure of the ticking clock. The countdown of my life as I know it, while the moon inches into the sky. I feel my limbs morph, change.

Blaxton pushes his body harder against my own. "You're nearly mine, beautiful," he whispers in my ear. I equally love and loathe his words, fighting the new alien feeling of ownership, of powerlessness against my will. I know, with absolute certainty, I will be his. I feel the moon pulling at lung and liver, despite him killing Grandma. Despite my loathing and hurt and pain. Despite my vendetta and revenge. The moon is washing it all away and I can't stop it.

I am losing myself.

Falling…

Falling…

Woolsey growls, and he doesn't have to shift into a wolf for me to know his hackles are up.

"Stand down, Woolsey," Blaxton warns, moving in front of me—protecting his spoils.

Woolsey dares a step forward.

"You will never have her," growls Blaxton as the full moon hits her highest point in the sky. *Those* words from *his* mouth slice and stab my soul. A pain, something to cling to as I fall into something new. Falling into animal power and instincts and wild, wild thoughts.

You will never have her.

I grip it with my mind, grip the cruel memories the words evoke as I lose all other sense of *me*.

Trapped, paralysed in my body as I brace against a noise I cannot escape—the curdling of Grandma's blood stuck in her ravaged throat as she died.

I howl.

I change.

I see the mean, greedy glint in Blaxton's eyes— he sees me as his.

He morphs. The white wolf with a question mark on his back and lust in his mind.

But I too have something on my mind.

Revenge.

I pounce, fur and fang, my body light and agile

as air. It is no longer Blaxton's heart I desire, but his throat. I latch on. Snarling, ripping, pulling—despite his yelps, and moans, and empty eyes losing their golden glow. His blood tastes as good as a debt paid in full and I feast in the retribution.

"Red! Red, please, stop."

And I do stop, breath heaving as I turn.

Woolsey, with his greedy eyes. No. Mistaken. I feel it now, an instinct. A knowing in my animal bones. They were never greedy, they were, what?

Longing.

And it all fits into place.

Woolsey turning up at Blaxton's cabin when the ravaged beast feasted on Betsy the old, helpless carthorse.

The warning at the funeral, 'Be careful. Be very careful.'

The stand-off at the doctor's house.

Saving me from a pack attack.

He wasn't watching me with greed, but with concern. With fear. With... my shoulder drop as the most innate human emotion pulls at my animal heart.

Love.

He was always looking out for me. Always trying to protect me. From Blaxton—from *myself*.

I pounce, shape shifting as I pound into Woolsey's arms, knocking us both to the ground. And with blood stained lips, we kiss.

The universe suddenly makes sense. I feel it beating with my half human half animal heart. Comets surge, stars are born. The world spins, I feel it, and I feel my place within it.

Passion will kill you, love will keep you alive, I hear Grandma saying, a faint sound disappearing into my own thoughts. And I feel both now—love and passion... *and* life, surging through my animal veins.

And I hear Grandma's voice no more. She has gone, left me, content in the knowing. Content that her dying wish has been made.

Blaxton will never have me. Not now. Not ever.

I allow my thoughts of Grandma to fade. There are more important things than mourning the dead after all; loving the living.

And owning the curse. It's mine, all mine. Now *I* hold the power. My *bloodline* holds the power.

I am a victim no more.

THE END

GET YOUR FREE MOON BITTEN SWAG BAG!

If you enjoyed Moon Bitten, you might love the free swag bag, what's inside? Why not take a look right here!

https://www.angharadthompsonrees.com/moon-bitten-swag/

If you enjoyed this tale, you might love The Magic and Mage YA Fantasy Series.
Grab the 1st in series for free here!
Witch Hearts

https://www.angharadthompsonrees.com/free-witch-hearts/

ABOUT THE AUTHOR

Angharad Thompson Rees is an author and scriptwriter, writing across a broad spectrum of genres and age groups; from children's and middle grade fantasy, to young adult gothic horror. She is an award winning spoken word poet and creator of whimsical illustrations and creative journals. Find out more at:

www.angharadthompsonrees.com

facebook.com/angharadthompsonrees

twitter.com/1angharad_rees

instagram.com/angharadthompsonrees

Printed in Great Britain
by Amazon

43093829R00067